this
little ORCHARD
book belongs to
....
....
D0416673

ORCHARD BOOKS
96 Leonard Street, London EC2A 4XD
Orchard Books Australia
32/45-51 Huntley Street, Alexandria NSW 2015
1 84362 217 3
First published in Great Britain in 2000
This edition published in 2003

A CIP catalogue record for this book is available from the British Library.
Printed in Italy

Freddie goes on an aeroplane

Nicola Smee

little ORCHARD

We're going to Spain
on an AEROPLANE
to see my Uncle Teddy.

We've never flown before!

At the airport we show our tickets and passport.

But before we can board the aeroplane our handluggage has to be x-rayed.

When our seatbelts are fastened the aeroplane gets ready for take-off and the engines

ROAR!

Then up, up, up we go…

Look! Look Bear! We're on top of the clouds!

. . . up into the clear blue sky.

The hostess gives us some
crayons and paper.

And later, some drink and food
in a little plastic tray.

yum yum

When we start to land we have sweets to suck to stop our ears going 'pop'!

Pass me one, please Bear

I show the hostess my pictures
and she says she hopes I fly
on her aeroplane again.

I will !

Then we have to wait for our luggage to come round on the carousel.

Look Mum! Look Bear!
Uncle Teddy's
over there!
EXIT
Freddie